Incognito

by Jack Lennox

illustrated by Scott Brooks

HOUGHTON MIFFLIN HARCOURT
School Publishers

Copyright © by Houghton Mifflin Harcourt Publishing Company

Printed in China

ISBN-13: 978-0-547-01764-8
ISBN-10: 0-547-01764-2

14 15 16 17 0940 19 18 17 16
4500569761

"I still remember the day I got it. One of my friends in the old neighborhood was moving and had to sell most of his things. As soon as I saw the cover, I jumped. This was the only issue I didn't have."

Ava Madera's father was standing in front of a file cabinet in his study. Its four drawers contained his prized comic book collection. He had started telling Ava about his collection earlier that morning at breakfast, when he had seen the picture of The Brick on her box of breakfast cereal.

Dad had told the story again—how he had fallen in love with comics as a boy… how he had first learned about collecting… how he diligently worked his paper route for years to support his hobby… how he learned which comics were most valuable… how exciting it was to locate a comic he'd been searching for… how exhilarating it was to witness the launch of a new series.

Every once in a while, Ava's father would pause, lingering over a folder in one of the drawers and showing her a complete series. Then he'd go on. He was looking for something. When he finally found the folder he wanted, he grinned broadly and turned to Ava. "Here's the folder. I loved this series as soon as I saw the cover. Something about the drawings, maybe."

Ava knew which series he was talking about—*Incognito*. Her father had told her about this amazing superhero before. Incognito could actually mold his facial bones and change his skin—jaw, nose, forehead, skin color, mouth, everything. This allowed him to change his entire appearance. He could become a square-jawed marine, a suntanned cowboy, a round-faced clerk, or a long-faced farmer.

Incognito could make himself look older or younger, male or female, almost instantly. This meant he could go anywhere without being recognized—that was the source of his name, *Incognito*. Incognito could infiltrate any organization, and if anyone identified him, he could change into someone else. He always defeated the villains.

Ava looked over at her father fondly. When he talked about comics, especially his favorite episodes, his face glowed. Ava didn't really share his enthusiasm for comic books; she preferred mystery novels.

Still, she loved listening to her dad's stories, so she sat down beside him as he brought the folder to the couch. She leaned forward as he gently took the *Incognito* comics, one by one, out of the folder.

There were only a few comic books, and each was carefully stored in a shiny glassine envelope.

Ava's dad had explained earlier that Tony Revere, the artist and creator, had produced *Incognito* for only two years. That's what made each issue so valuable. And Dan Madera had all eight precious issues. His favorite was #3, the first special book he'd found at his friend's sale. It featured Incognito breaking up a ring of thieves who stole precious jewels from royal tombs.

He took each comic out of the folder and, without removing any from their clear envelopes, showed his daughter the covers. The cover art was beautifully drawn, she had to admit. "And here…" he started, but then his face darkened, and he took back the comic Ava was holding. He leafed rapidly through the others. He counted the books once, then again. There were only seven books! One issue was missing. It was #3, his favorite.

Dan Madera leaped up, dashed to the file cabinet, and thumbed through every folder. Ava watched, holding her breath. *Please let him find issue #3*, she thought. But it was no use. The precious #3 was gone.

"That comic must be somewhere," Ava said weakly. "Did you look through each folder? Maybe it's stuck at the bottom of the drawer."

Sighing, her dad shook his head and said, "That issue must have gotten lost when we moved. I wish I could remember who brought my comic collection to our new house." Dad was still holding the *Incognito* folder, looking incredibly sad.

"Don't worry," Ava tried to console him. "I'm sure it will turn up."

But the comic didn't turn up, not even when Ava's mother looked through the entire file cabinet herself. And Mom held the record for finding things that were missing.

Ava decided right then and there that she could not let her father down. She would find him another *Incognito* #3. How hard could it be to find a comic book?

Ava developed her plan that evening. First, she would talk with her friend Marcy's older brother, Peter. He could sometimes be a pain, like all teenagers, but he knew everything about comic books. Then she would search the Internet. You could find anything there.

Many people sold comics on Internet auction sites, and she could even go to garage sales. After all, her father had found his first *Incognito* #3 at a garage sale. After that, assuming she still hadn't found the issue, she would search out comic book stores—there had to be some in Galveston.

The next day, Ava went to visit Marcy and asked Peter about comic books. He told Ava about several comic book stores and even said she could come with him to a store next week.

"Check out the Internet in the meantime," he advised her. "There are a million websites that sell comics." Peter wasn't so sure about garage sales, though.

"Most of what you'd find there is probably pretty beat up," he confided. "You might have better luck on the Internet. Try to find a reputable collectors' website."

Peter also told her about a magazine that listed comic book sales. If *Incognito* #3 had sold recently, he said, the magazine would tell her how much it had sold for.

"Where can I find a magazine like that?" Ava asked him.

"I've got an issue from last year," Peter said. "I'll go get it now."

When he brought the magazine out, Marcy looked at Ava with amazement. Her brother was rarely this helpful! But unfortunately, when Peter checked the magazine for *Incognito*, he found that no copies of #3 had been sold. But a #1 *had* sold, and it had sold for a lot.

"Wow," Peter whistled, impressed. "It sold for $45, and that's pretty pricey."

As Peter talked, Ava listened intently, making mental notes. When she got home, she found a notebook and carefully wrote down everything she remembered. Peter had told her that a #3 ought to be about the same price as a #1, maybe a little more, maybe a little less. That night after she finished her homework, she went online and searched for "comic books."

Once she started searching, Ava felt stunned. First, she had no idea there were so many different comics. She knew about *Superbat* and *The Brick* and *Rubberneck* and *Millidigit*.

But these were only the "Golden Agers." There were thousands more, featuring superheroes of every description—*Prototype* and *Chrysalizzy*, *Octopus Eye* and *Bole the Barbarian*, *Blue Bison* and *Terminalis*. Then there were the foreign ones like *Tout Neuf* and *Archeo*. There were comics from movies, too. There were comics about prehistoric creatures and futuristic robots. There were *manga* comics from Japan. All were being bought and sold every day, every hour, online.

All at once, Ava spotted the one she wanted—*Incognito*. Her heart was pounding as she clicked on the icon. The issues available were 1, 2, 4, 7, 8—but no #3. "Just my luck," she sighed in disappointment.

She typed in another website address, but on this site, *Incognito* was not even listed.

Incognito #1 .... Very Fine $50

Incognito #2 .... Fine $32

Incognito #4 .... Very Fine $27

Incognito #7 .... Near Mint $25

Incogniton #8 .... Very Good $8

Ava continued for another hour. Her brain was getting blurry, so she finally stopped and went to sleep. Naturally, she dreamed about superheroes.

By the end of the week, Ava had checked every website she could find. She found several more #1's for sale, all for about $50. She also found several #5's and just about every other issue, but not one #3 appeared. She was pretty discouraged when she called Marcy on Saturday morning. Peter was there, too, and he agreed to take both of them to his favorite comics store that afternoon.

Comix was located on Mission Avenue in downtown Galveston. Saturday was its busiest day. What amazed Ava were the differences in the people. There were dozens of kids her age, but there were older shoppers, too. Some looked like students from the university, while others looked like retired professors. Still others seemed about her dad's age. And everyone was avidly thumbing through stacks and stacks of comic books.

While Peter pushed his way to the section he liked best, Ava and Marcy waited for the clerk, who had spiky hair and wore a colorful T-shirt with a Bole the Barbarian drawing on it. Ava and Marcy tried not to giggle. They told him what they wanted.

"Whoa, *Incognito*," he said, looking at them curiously. "I haven't come across that name in months. Where'd you hear about it?"

"My dad," Ava told him. "That's his favorite series, and I want to get him #3."

"Ah," he said, and again looked at them with a curious expression on his face. Then he said confidentially, "Tell you what—we don't have it in stock right now, but I maybe could find you one. It might take a week, so could you come back?"

Feeling hopeful, Ava said that they sure could.

On their way home, Ava and Marcy told Peter about the clerk. Peter warned them about two things. "First, make sure all the pages are there. Second, watch out for fakes. I've never had any trouble at that store, but these days, with computers and color printers, you never know. It's easy to forge comics. Take a good look at your dad's comics and don't buy anything that doesn't appear to have the same quality."

That week, Ava continued to look on the Internet, but she still had no luck. She even went to a garage sale down the street, but there were no comic books for sale. She was beginning to feel as if she were looking for a needle in a haystack.

On Saturday, she and Marcy took the train to Galveston. The Comix store was packed, as usual. When the clerk was free, they asked him if he'd had any luck finding the comic. He grinned and then reached under his counter, pulling out a glassine envelope with a comic inside.

There it was! *Incognito* #3. "It's in mint condition," he stated in an authoritative voice. Ava knew by now what that meant. This copy of #3 was nearly perfect, like a coin just made at the mint. Her dad would be totally amazed.

"Could we look at it?" Ava asked shakily.

"Sure. Just be careful. No smudges, huh?" And he eyed their fingers.

Ava thumbed through the pages one by one. She tried to follow the story, looking at all the pictures; she wanted to make sure every page was there. The first two chapters looked complete, but then, about halfway through the final chapter, Ava noticed a gap—the story didn't track. Alarmed, she looked more carefully at the cover and realized that the cover paper seemed different from the covers she'd seen at home.

Ava whispered to Marcy, "I think something is wrong." She pointed to the gap and at the cover, as Marcy nodded her head.

They had agreed earlier that if something seemed wrong, they'd just say they needed time to think about their purchase. Peter had warned them not to directly accuse anyone of selling fake comics.

"This issue looks pretty good," Ava told the clerk. "But I need to think it over. It's more expensive than I thought it would be."

The clerk's face flashed annoyance. Kids! He snapped, "Suit yourself," quickly putting the envelope back beneath the counter.

Ava picked up a card on the counter and said she'd call. Then she and Marcy scooted out the door. A block away, Ava stopped and blurted out, "Oh my goodness, did you see the look on his face? I thought we were in trouble!" Breathless, Marcy agreed, and they ran the rest of the way to the station. On the train, they could not stop laughing at themselves. "Why should we be afraid? *He's* the crook!"

Marcy called her brother from the train. "Guess what? I think the clerk at Comix just tried to sell us a fake!" She couldn't get the words out fast enough. "Something was missing from the story, and the cover looked like it was printed on cheap paper!"

"That sure sounds like a fake," Peter confirmed. "Good thing you looked carefully at each page. Trying to return the book would have been a nightmare!" Peter sounded relieved that the girls had taken his advice.

Now, though, Ava's hopes of finding *Incognito* #3 really plunged. Phone calls to every other comic book store in the area turned up nothing, and online auction sites turned up nothing as well. She had nearly given up.

A few evenings later, Ava's mother was looking for some summer clothes that she hadn't seen since their move. "I wonder if we left them at Grandma's?" she said.

Ava's mind leaped—Grandma's! Their old house had been right next door to Grandma's. Hadn't they left some boxes in Grandma's attic?

That Sunday, Ava and her mother visited Grandma. It always felt strange being back in the old neighborhood, but Ava didn't spend time thinking about that. While her mother chatted with Grandma, Ava ran straight up to the attic. She found some boxes labeled with her mother's writing. One said, *Photos, books, mags—Keep at Grandma's*.

Ava quickly cut through the tape and opened the box. Inside she found old travel magazines. She stopped and smiled when she saw some photos of her family at the beach. More photos. Old flyers. A dead spider. She was getting near the bottom. *Another dead end*, she thought.

Then her heart stopped. There, edged under one of the bottom flaps of the box, a glassine envelope peeked out. She lifted up the flap and carefully pulled out the envelope. Inside was a comic book.

Slowly and gingerly, she removed the book from its protective cover. Her heart beat fast. Was it—yes, it was *Incognito* #3! The precious issue wasn't lost after all! Someone, maybe Mom or Grandma, had put it in the wrong box. Ava skipped down the stairs, grinning.

That night after dinner, as her father was making
coffee, Ava came down the stairs with the comic book held
behind her back. "Guess what I found today?"

He smiled and joked, "A new galaxy?"

"Better than that," she announced.

"Then it must be really special."

"It is," Ava replied. She slowly drew the *Incognito* #3
from behind her back and placed it on the table. Her father
looked stunned.

She let her father go through every possibility. "You *bought* this? How did you find one? On the Internet? It's too expensive—I'll give you the money. Just look at this… I forgot how beautiful the drawings are. Have you looked at the drawings? Revere was inspired by Beninno, you know. Did I tell you that? Wow, just look at this gorgeous detail. I've really missed this!"

"I know," Ava said.

"But where…? How…?" he asked.

"At Grandma's," Ava told him, laughing. "It was there all the time, in her attic."

"At Grandma's," her father marveled. "How simple! Just like that."

"Yeah, simple," Ava grinned—and winked happily at her mother.

Responding

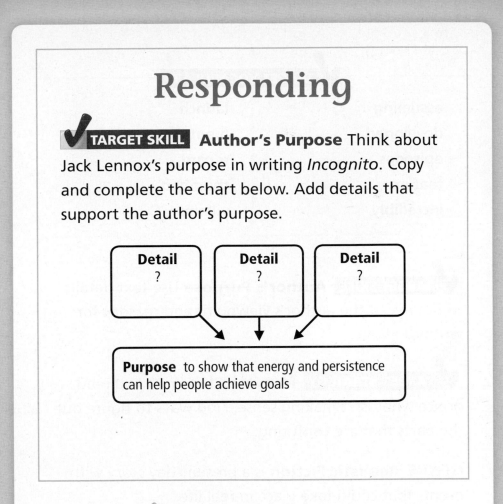

✔ **TARGET SKILL** **Author's Purpose** Think about Jack Lennox's purpose in writing *Incognito*. Copy and complete the chart below. Add details that support the author's purpose.

Detail	Detail	Detail
?	?	?

Purpose to show that energy and persistence can help people achieve goals

Write About It

Text to Self Think about a time when you or someone you know lost and then found a treasured item. Write a letter to a friend that describes what happened.

✔ **TARGET SKILL** **Author's Purpose** Use text details to figure out the author's viewpoint and reasons for writing.

✔ **TARGET STRATEGY** **Monitor/Clarify** As you read, notice what isn't making sense. Find ways to figure out the parts that are confusing.

GENRE **Realistic Fiction** is a present-day story with events that could take place in real life.